Role Model Ricky's Big Birthday Bash

Written by
Jeremy & Janel Miller

AuthorHouse™
1663 Liberty Drive
Bloomington, IN 47403
www.authorhouse.com
Phone: 1 (800) 839-8640

Published by AuthorHouse 8/28/2015

Library of Congress Control Number: 2015913358

ISBN: 978-1-5049-3229-5 (sc)
ISBN: 978-1-5049-3231-8 (hc)
ISBN: 978-1-5049-3230-1 (e)

Library of Congress Control Number: 2015913358

Print information available on the last page.

This book is printed on acid-free paper.

authorHOUSE®

Dedication

This book is dedicated to each of our parents who taught us the importance of strong family values, hard work, and responsibility. Thank you for raising us to be the people we are today.

Jeremy & Janel

This is Ricky. Today is his birthday.

Ricky wanted a big party with all of his friends.

His mom told him he could only have a party if he was a good role model. A role model is someone who has good behavior and a positive attitude, listens to his or her parents, and is nice to others.

Ricky has been very good this year by listening to his parents, sharing with his friends, and being nice to others.

Since Ricky has been a good role model, today he is having a big party!

Ricky and his friends had lunch, built a fort, and played basketball.

Then it was time for some birthday cake. All of Ricky's friends sang "Happy Birthday" to him, and he blew out the candles.

Finally, it was the time Ricky had been waiting for: presents! He has been a super good role model, so he got lots of presents from his friends and parents.

Ricky got a book, a football, some clothes, and a new train set! He could not wait to play with everything, especially the train set.

Ricky asked his mom and dad politely if he could open the new train set. "Since you asked so nicely, we can open it now," said his dad. Ricky was very excited!

Ricky's friends wanted to play with the train set too.

At first, Ricky was not sure he wanted to share his new train set. He thought to himself, *Hmm, I could push or hit my friends or even yell and scream really loud ... but that would not be a good decision.*

I could throw the train set at my friends, but that would not be very nice either. Plus, someone could get hurt.

Or I could share my new train set and play nicely with my friends.

Now that would be a good decision!

Ricky shared his new train set with his friends, and they even helped him build a cool track.

Ricky's mom said, "Thank you for being a good role model by sharing with your friends. That was a great choice."

Ricky showed he was a role model by making good decisions, being nice, and sharing with his friends instead of pushing, hitting, yelling, screaming, or throwing his train set.

Before Ricky's friends went home, he gave each of them a gift to thank them for coming to his party.

After his friends went home, Ricky thanked his mom and dad for the birthday party and gave them a big hug and a kiss. Then it was time for bed.

Ricky brushed his teeth, read a bedtime story with his dad, and went to sleep. It was a great day for Role Model Ricky!

Senator pens children's book

Submitted photo

■ Senator Jeremy Miller and his wife Janel received a lot of feedback on their new children's book "Role Model Ricky's Big Birthday Bash" from their sons, Drew, Luke and Tom.

CPSIA information can be obtained
at www.ICGtesting.com
Printed in the USA
LVOW05s1158241115
463988LV00007B/29/P

9 781504 932295